BLOOD LEGENDS

UNDEAD

KIM PETERSEN

DEDICATION

This book is dedicated to lovers of new energy, beauty and creatures of the night – this series is for dreamers.

CONTENTS

EXCERPT - BLOOD LEGENDS
BOOK ONE

ACKNOWLEDGMENTS

I initially wrote this book as an introduction to my *Blood Legends* world which was written in the same world albeit fifty years in the future from when this story takes place.

Alas, I am continuing to charter Jett's story because I think it will be really cool to explore the very beginning – why the notorious vampire clans – the Mysticus and the Cruentus - came to be bitter rivals, and why they fear the emergence of an elusive and mystical relic.

Stay tuned for the next book set to release following *Undead – Blood Legends: Rebirth,* as well as more instalments from the *Blood Legends* series.

I wish to thank editors Dan Moore and Kay Bolden from Medium publication, P.S. I Love You for publishing *Undead* as weekly instalments on their amazing corner of the web. Their support has been encouraging and humbling.

A huge thanks to my editor, Paul Vander Loos who teaches me endlessly while enjoying fruitless and (amusing) attempts at anticipating where I'll take my stories.

Patti Roberts for her beautiful artworks and even more admirable energy.

Xavier Eastenbrick for his amazing ways and unrelenting support – the world needs more like you. I am forever grateful.

And to you; who has picked up this book to discover a new vampire world: *Blood Legends*. I hope you will enjoy it as much as I have creating it.

Thank you. Thank you. Thank you.

Kim xx

BLOOD LEGENDS

UNDEAD

USA Today Bestselling Author

KIM PETERSEN

What if Saving Humanity Meant Facing Your Greatest Fears?

A deadly virus has claimed the lives of millions and ravaged the earth. Human survivors spend their days and nights fighting to stay alive in a world now owned by vampires.

Jett's plans to get further off-grid fall apart when his woman suddenly disappears at the hands of the hawkers – the most deplorable and dangerous humans to survive the apocalypse.

Now, Jett is forced to confront evil head-on as he faces choices that he never dreamed possible. Can he survive long enough to retrieve his woman before she is slaughtered? Or will he succumb to the bloody wrath of the Undead?

Undead is a new urban fantasy set in a post-apocalyptic world from bestselling author Kim Petersen, the first book in the *Blood Legends* series.

FOOTPRINTS

"*D*id you ever want to step into someone else's feet?"

I tore my eyes from the gulls screeching above the waves that crashed against the jagged rocks, their wings beating against the briny air as they swooped the water's surface looking for a meal. A faint smile played over my lips.

"Don't you mean shoes?"

The breeze captured Scarla's platinum locks as amber eyes settled on me. Her smile was as meek as mine, dissolving just as fast when she dropped her gaze to grab a handful of sand. My throat restricted. The wind instantly carried a chord of torment as I watched her.

"No." She allowed the golden grains to fall from

between her fingers. She raised her chin toward the sky and squeezed her eyes shut. "Thousands of footprints have marked this beach over just as many years; I'd give anything to step in any one of them."

My stomach hollowed.

"But then you wouldn't be here with me in this moment." I reached to catch a tear as it splashed over her cheek, folding my palm against her smooth skin while my gaze melted into her. She was all I saw in a disintegrating world. She was everything. "You would rather be elsewhere?"

She leaned her chin into my palm, her lashes dewy when she met my stare.

"Yes, with you, Jett."

"Where should we go?"

My gaze instantly fell to her lips when she smiled. Pale pink and plump. They reminded me of blossoms and lifted my heart in much the same way. She had a way of doing that. She had a way of bringing me undone.

"Florence." She pulled away from my touch, combing a hand through unruly hair as it wisped across her face. Her white blouse rippled and clung to her breasts.

"Ah, you want to immerse yourself in some Italian Renaissance, Bella donna? Where should we start? The Galleria degli Uffizi?"

She laughed.

"That will do just fine, signor. We'll spend our days exploring galleries, eating crostini di fegato and drinking chianti while we marvel at the architectural masterpieces. Afterwards, we will put on our best threads and go to the opera."

I feigned a frown.

"The opera? Hmm..."

"What?" She gave me a gentle nudge. "I'm sure you can conjure up your inner-aristocrat for a few hours if need be."

"Only for you, Bella donna."

I shifted, positioning myself behind her on the sand and pulling her between my legs so that her back molded against my chest. I wrapped my arms around her, burying my nose near her ear and breathing in her scent. She stiffened, her voice barely audible over the sound of the rumbling waters.

"Do you think the virus has spread that far?"

I shrugged.

"If it has, we'll get love-drunk on chianti at the opera with them. I hear the undead love high society."

"That's not funny."

"I'm not laughing." I pressed my lips against her temple. She tasted salty. *Sensually salty.* My voice was husky when I spoke next. "Can't we just pretend a little longer?"

She arched her neck so that her throat stretched beneath the afternoon sun. Her eyes closed as she leaned further into me, reaching to claw her fingers through the dark hair curling at my nape. I wanted her now, but I knew this wasn't the time nor the place for intimacy. We were alone on the beach, yet that could change at any moment. People were seldom friendly these days. Especially those that we call the hawkers.

My gaze drifted toward the horizon as I held her in my arms. If I could pretend on anything, it would be any place but here as long as she was by my side. It would be some place where the Vampiric virus ravaging the earth couldn't reach.

They say everything happens for a reason. Yet, I could think of no justifiable reason for the horror our world had become. Almost overnight, the lives of millions of people worldwide had turned into a living nightmare. A harsh reality where those infected by the virus feasted on humanity during the dark hours. Now, it was the kindred that were fast staking supremacy over the earth; humans had become the minority.

My thoughts shifted to my daughter, Avila, who we'd left behind in our hidden cottage; the meager refuge we'd sought after fleeing the city when it became obvious that I could no longer help contain the rapid spread of the virus. We were among the lucky ones who got out just in time.

"We should get back to the cottage," I said, knowing that she wasn't ready to leave. It wasn't often that we stole time away from the cottage. I'd come here for her. Sometimes, she needed to dream.

She squirmed in my arms, swinging around to face me. Her brows creased.

"Just a little longer? I want to trek through some footprints before we go back." She motioned toward the sand etched with shallow prints. "Will you join me?"

I held her gaze, smiling behind the pain of all I knew she'd suffered and lost to the outbreak. She'd lost her little boy at the hands of a vampire. I shook my head.

"Go find your rainbow, Bella donna. I'll wait here."

"Okay." Her eyes deepened against the blue of mine as her lips slightly parted and she leaned toward me. I groaned inwardly as the sweet taste of promises to come found my mouth with her kiss. They say that the eyes are the gateway to the soul. I think lips are the same for the body. She pulled away and leapt to her feet, casting me a grin. "I'll be ten minutes. You can watch my rainbow from here."

I scanned the beach again, pushing away the apprehension that shadowed my every waking hour.

"Stay where I can see you."

My words were swallowed in the wind and the space between us as she walked toward the shore, but I knew she wouldn't wander far from me. She was more than aware of the lurking dangers in the form of hawkers. They were the ones who polluted the daylight hours by terrorizing the survivors. The profane remains of humanity who relished the aftermath with unspeakable acts of violence. Thankfully, we hadn't encountered any hawkers this far from the city. Still, you can never be too vigilant.

I watched Scarla for a few minutes as she stomped between prints, and looking back at me every now and then, smiling. She was safe enough that I took a breath and sprawled back into the sand. The warm grains cushioned my head as I closed my eyes beneath the sun, inviting the false sense of well-being its rays provided.

For the millionth time since the arrival of the V-Virus, I thought about the continuation of life. It isn't until you are faced with endless death and chaos that you realize the earth will stop for nothing and no one. There are no free rides out of here when evil comes calling. No help lines to pull you from the brink of insanity.

A few moments passed and I became aware of the breeze gathering speed, catching clumps of my hair as the sand sprayed like sharp needles against my skin. Suddenly, I felt cold all over, the breeze blowing in a sense of dread. I sat up abruptly, looking back to the place I'd last spotted Scarla scouring the shoreline but she wasn't there.

Scarla?

My heart thumped hard against my chest as I stood up and scanned the beach. I was confronted by a stretch of bronze sand in every direction as far as the eye could see, barren of life apart from the gulls that squawked and hovered above the waves licking the shore.

I could feel my head begin to spin as I called her name, but my words were instantly stolen by the wind as panic gripped me and my feet dug into the sand to seek out her footprints. Prints that I knew would haunt me for the rest of my days.

2

THE HAWKERS

A thick cloud of dust billowed above the road behind me as I slammed my foot against the accelerator of the pickup. Any other day, I would have taken extreme care to disguise the sound of the engine, much less leave an obvious path of smut leading toward the cottage. But today wasn't any other day. Today Scarla had vanished without a trace.

Hawkers. It had to be. But how they managed to slip past me to grab Scarla undetected in a matter of minutes was beyond my comprehension. And all without so much as a sound from her to alarm me.

Since when did those lowlife pilferers possess such stealthy tactics?

My thoughts harrowed over the severe truth. *Since*

vermin infected our streets and claimed most of the population.

Anarchy and destruction have a way of bringing out the best and the worst in humanity. Eventually, you cultivate the ability to ignore the suffering when desperation becomes second nature to every surviving human. But ignorance isn't an option when you're targeted by the wicked.

My knuckles whitened as I gripped the steering wheel and the tires slid over the rough terrain, just missing one of the dense and twisted tree trunks that fringed the road. I was covered in sweat and a thin layer of grime from searching the grassed hinterlands near the beach for signs of her. My face stung with the moisture that clung to the scratches I knew marked my face, but I barely felt it. It was all I could do to keep it together as I raced back to the cottage to get what I needed before starting back out to look for her.

Damn it! How could I be so foolish? How?

I let loose a barrage of four-letter words, fighting to keep control of what little resolve remained. I should have known better than to yield to Scarla's desire to escape the confines of the cottage. *Dying dreams on broken wings cannot fly.* There is no room left in this world for the dreamers. They were poached the moment the virus murdered most of humanity.

Avila was already out front and standing at the foot of the cottage porch stairs when the truck skidded around the final bend to emerge into the clearing. Her aqua eyes narrowed toward me while her usually chiseled features scrunched beneath the thick tawny hair framing her face. As I yanked the parking brake lever and moved to get out of the truck, her olive complexion paled as she rushed closer and pulled on the truck door to face me.

"Dad?" Her gaze drifted beyond me to the empty truck cabin. My breath felt like steel when she looked back at me. "Wha ... where's Scarla?"

Her voice quavered but I could barely look at her. I shook my head fast before climbing out of the truck and pushing past her. I marched toward the cottage, bounding up the few stairs leading to the front door as she raced after me.

"Dad, stop!" She grabbed my arm, sinking her nails into my flesh as I reached the threshold. It was difficult to tame my racing mind when I turned to face her. Even more difficult to form the words I knew I had to say. Her brows dipped over a pinched expression. She clutched onto me. "What happened? Where is she?"

"I don't know, she vanished."

Her jaw gaped as I tore my arm from her and walked into the cottage. It was a modest dwelling with timber floors and burnt orange curtains that Scarla thought gave the place a cheerful vibe. I'd never agreed with that notion. I hated those curtains.

But curtains were the last thing on my mind as I stomped through the cluttered space that passed for the sitting area, heading for the room at the end of the short hall that stocked our supplies. The small room was filled with stockpiles of canned and dried foods, loads of water, kerosene, and piles of spare bedding among other things. It was here that I'd kept the few weapons I had managed to salvage before deserting the city.

Admittedly, there wasn't a whole lot, and none of it would be of any use in the face of a vampire. Humans, on the other hand, could bleed when facing the blunt end of the few rusty hunting knives I'd collected. There was also a small-bladed axe, a cleaver and my prized possession, a machete that I used frequently to cut and gather firewood. I'd heard machetes were particularly useful for cutting limbs in addition to wood. Somehow, I got the feeling I might soon discover how to dismember a hawker or two. It was limbs and blood that I craved right now.

The blades were discreetly stacked on the shelf in the corner behind rows of water bricks, cans of fuel and oil, and dozens of bottles of bleach and candles. I began pulling them out as Avila burst into the room, stopping just short of me. I ignored her glare as her arms outstretched to take the knives as I pried them from the shelf.

"Hawkers?" Her boots squeaked on the timber floor as she swung around to place the weapons on an old coffee table pushed against the shelves.

"I didn't see them."

She took the cleaver from me, catching my gaze with solemn eyes.

"What are you going to do?"

"I'm going to find the bastards and cut off their limbs, that's what I'm going to do." I swung my gaze from her and reached for the machete, stiffening when I felt her hand on my arm.

"It's too late, dad. She's gone. We can't get her back."

My entire body felt as if an explosion was shredding every organ. But my heart fought ceaselessly against the onslaught. As much as I loved my 22-year-old daughter, those were the words I didn't want to hear.

I dropped my chin and sighed, the machete heavy in my hand as I allowed the blade to swing to my side. The inside of my head throbbed against my temple. It was pain that consumed me as Avila's hard stare begged for my acknowledgment. The moments stood as still as a tomb on a starless night. They were the same moments that forever sealed our fate like an impenetrable vault.

When I looked back at her, it was the pain that thickened my voice.

"I won't let her go, Avila. I've already lost too much.' I shook my head. "I looked away from her for only a moment and they snatched her away. I have to get her back."

Avila's jaw twisted. She gnawed on her bottom lip before gesturing toward the lone window in the airless room.

"Okay, but there's nothing we can do right now; it's almost nightfall." I was about to protest when she stopped me with a flash of a palm. "Listen dad, we can't do this alone. You can't do it alone. They'll kill you on sight. We need to contact Michal. We need help."

Michal was our sole connection to what little life remained in the city. We'd been work colleagues at the Norbury Blood Research Center for more than two decades. He was one of the most gifted hematologists I'd ever met and had chosen to stay in the city to search for a cure for the V-Virus, working with a group of vigilante scientists in an underground laboratory.

Our communication with Michal was sparse and not always reliable, considering that the only means of contact rested solely on old CB radio transmitter. We'd agreed to reach out to one another only when it was necessary. Scarla was more than necessary, but what could he do? He was a few hours' drive away and I had no idea if he could handle a blade.

I swung my gaze toward the window, noting the diminishing light spreading through a gap in the curtains. Honestly, the way I felt, I could not care less about the threat of the kindred if it meant I could find Scarla and bring her home. But I was aware my thoughts weren't rational at that moment. There was Avila; I had to protect her too.

Reaching out to Michal couldn't hurt. Perhaps he could stay with Avila while I got this under control. My fingers clenched the machete handle as I glanced back at her, ready to concede when a loud knock thumped against the cottage door. The sound of my name spoken by an unfamiliar and gnarly voice reverberated through the flimsy walls.

What the hell?

Avila's eyes widened. I motioned for her to stay put as I gripped the machete and raced to the front of the cottage, edging along the wall of the sitting room to steal a glance through the curtains at the yard. My blood drained to my feet as I caught sight of a group of hawkers spreading across the clearing and leaning against the timber porch frame.

There must have been about fifteen of them wearing ragged leather jackets above grimy jeans and carrying an array of long blades and rusted chains between frayed fingerless gloves. The voice called again; the sound of my name grating against my churning gut. I steeled myself, taking the few steps toward the door before flinging it open.

Stained teeth greeted me with a wry grin that split between wiry ginger whiskers. His tall, solid frame filled my vision as he toyed with a switch blade and cocked his chin to the side. Dark eyes bore into me above pockmarked skin.

"Ah, you're home! How fortunate that we caught you at the witching hour."

My eyes flashed dangerously.

"What do you want?"

He laughed, a few of his cronies joining in when he leered their way. He turned back at me.

"You're asking the wrong question, my friend." He leaned closer, his breath hot and rancid in my face. "I have what you want. The question you should be asking is how bad do you want it."

3

SUN

Forty-eight hours. That was the deal offered by the hawkers if I wanted to keep Scarla breathing. She now had a ransom on her head – a blood-ransom.

Myths and legends always seem to accompany major change. In a new world where blood ruled, it was blood that had become our most valuable commodity. Scarla's life had just become dependent upon a few drops of rare blood. Blood represented power to its possessor, and I was uncertain I could produce the payoff.

Avila lifted her head from the cradle of her arm and yawned beside me in the pickup cabin. I glanced at her before looking back to the road that stretched ahead in an endless brutal strip as we sped toward the city. It was brutal for the bloodshed it had silently witnessed and for that which dwelled at its end. We were headed back into vampire territory.

"Are you okay?" My voice was as rigid as the stupidity of the question, but I knew she was good at disguising her fear. My little tough nugget wasn't always as brawny as she made out. Still, her courage in the face of the epidemic was admirable.

She snorted and gazed out the passenger window. Fields of rotted vegetation and wild grasslands swayed beneath the morning sun, blurring the passing landscape.

"Of course." She looked back at me. "Is it really true, dad?"

"Is what true?"

"What the hawkers said about AB positive blood type. You've never mentioned it before. Can it transcend a vampire's supernatural powers?"

The sun's sharp heat already bit at my brow despite the early hour. When I lowered the truck window, the foul odor of spoiled crops instantly assaulted my senses. I flinched and tried not to gag.

"I wish I had the answers, Avila."

"Well, you of all people should know."

I flinched again, and this time, it wasn't because of the rotting crops. My eyes never left the road when I answered.

"It doesn't matter what I know or don't know. All that matters is that the hawkers believe it enough to keep Scarla hostage until I deliver it to them." I wiped my brow with the back of hand. My jaw clenched. "And that's exactly what I'm going to do."

Or die trying.

She was silent for a few beats, her fingers toying with one of the wooden stakes swaddled in a bag that lay on the bench seat between us. She sighed.

"Maybe Michal has the answers. Last night when you spoke to him, I heard him tell you he has one vial there at the lab. Surely, he's discovered something new by now? After all, you guys put in some grueling hours before ... the end."

She was referring to the intense blood research program I had participated in when there was still hope the epidemic could be controlled. Of course, we'd failed. But when delirium had struck near the end, so too did the mysterious tales begin to circulate about a blood type that could provide the supernatural with even more extraordinary powers. Alas, by that time, most of the city had fallen and with it, the remaining blood banks ransacked and gutted.

No one really knew where the legend surrounding the rare blood type had originated. Some say the collapse of humanity was an ironic twist of fate handed down by unseen higher forces. That our most vital lifeforce would prove to be our undoing. Those same folks foretold a future time of reckoning in the form of a blood legend. Whether there was truth to those mystifying predictions did not concern me. I wanted no part in this new world. Once I got Scarla back, I planned on taking my girls and getting further off grid. Blood legends and myths be damned.

"Dad?"

I glanced at Avila, catching her eyes tapering as the wind blew fast into the truck cabin. She pushed strands of dark hair from her face.

"Yeah?"

"If Michal has a vial of this rare blood, why would he give it up so readily for us?"

It was a valid question and one that had already crossed my mind. I'd managed to contact Michal after the hawkers had left the evening before. He had been pleased to hear from me, posing little protest when I filled him in on our current predicament and what I needed to get Scarla back. We'd left the cottage at first light with the promise of the blood we needed awaiting us in an underground city laboratory.

I pushed away the unease rippling through me and shrugged. Even as I spoke my next words, I wasn't sure I believed them.

"Why wouldn't he, Avila? Heck, he's been a part of our lives for over twenty years. I trust him."

She gave a half laugh.

"The concept of trust disintegrated when the city fell and vampires overtook the world." She turned away, speaking toward the black tarmac that stretched before us. "*You* were the one that taught me that."

Indeed, I was. It was something I'd drummed into both Scarla and Avila. Keeping the guards up and the barriers firmly erected was as important to withstanding the new world as the basic needs for survival. As it was, we were fortunate to have enough supplies stockpiled at the cottage to last several months if rationed carefully. And as far as trusting Michal, Avila could be right, but I had no choice but to pursue the blood and this was my only option.

I was about to voice as much when Avila gasped and jerked next to me, lifting her arm to gesture toward a lone figure appearing on the hazy black horizon.

"Up ahead, dad. Look!"

My skin flushed as I squinted beneath dark sunglasses. My mind whirled with possible scenarios. You don't often spot lone figures walking along the deserted highways. You don't stop to ask questions either. Yet, as we neared the solitary person hiking in the middle of the road, my thoughts were lost when she spun around to face us, the sun catching the length of her wild golden tresses while her long black dress flowed with her movements.

A woman?

My foot automatically eased off the accelerator and my breath quickened with my knotting belly. The air in the pickup thickened with decaying pungent offerings as we slowed. When the woman raised a palm to wave us down, I noticed the rucksack slung over one shoulder and the wooden stake she gripped by her side. The sound of Avila's voice was the next thing I heard over the rumbling truck motor.

"What are you doing? Don't stop for her, dad. Keep moving." Her eyes were like frantic storm clouds when I tore my gaze from the woman to meet her stare. She shook her head wildly. "It's got to be a trick."

I took a shallow breath and scanned the area, the pickup now only inching forward as I clutched the steering wheel. The roadside was a tangle of high weeds and twisted bramble that suffocated farm fences and boarded rising fields of sloping grasses. Anyone could be hiding in those shrubs. Anyone. Still, I felt compelled to press my foot on the brake as we drew closer.

"Is your door locked?" My voice was taut as I double checked my own door and wound up my window until only a few inches remained open.

Avila checked her door and gasped loudly. "Have you lost your mind?"

Perhaps I had lost my mind. Either that or it was fast deteriorating beneath the precarious nature of the unfolding events, but something compelled me to stop for this woman and I had no idea why. I didn't look at Avila as I began to veer alongside the woman, maintaining a crawl in the pickup.

"Keep vigilant." I reached for the machete that was propped next to me.

"Ha! A lot of good that's gonna be if we're ambushed with weapons. What if they have guns? You have lost all your marbles."

She fell silent when the woman smiled from between chafed lips and fell into step on my side of the pickup. Her blonde hair fell stringy over slim shoulders clad in a faded denim jacket worn over a red singlet. Grimy fingers adjusted a pair of dark sunglasses poised on a petite nose.

"Thanks for stopping." Her voice was as light as the breeze drifting off the unkempt, sleepy pastures. The cawing sounds of crows circling over the fields clung overhead like an ominous warning as I stopped the truck. She looked beyond me to Avila. "My name is Sun. I'm heading back to the city. Can I ride with you?"

My jaw tightened and I dropped my eyes to the

stake she clasped. A slight chill prickled my spine when I saw the dried blood that stained the end of the wooden stave.

"What's your business back in the city, Sun?"

She pushed her sunglasses to the top of her head and took a sharp breath. Eyes the color of gold peered at me from sunken sockets before she lowered her chin and swallowed hard.

"I'm going back for my daughter. I left her behind."

Avila scoffed next to me.

"Bullshit! If that's true, she's probably dead. Are you on a suicide mission or something?"

Sun's eyes instantly flew to Avila, and her lips quivered. She shook her head.

"Please. I have to know what happened to her."

Avila and I exchanged glances. Her lips pursed as she frowned at me. I gave a slight nod and ignored her look of disbelief as I turned back to Sun.

"Get in."

"So, what's your story, huh?" Avila glared at Sun sitting between us on the bench seat as we raced along the highway.

Sun shrugged; her fingers twisted in her lap. "What do you mean? My story isn't any different from anyone else's."

"Ha." Avila's lips curled as she indicated the stake leaning against the seat beside Sun. "I'm not buying the innocent act, *Sunny*. What's with the blood-soaked stake? Did you kill kindred?"

I glanced at Sun as her jaw squared while she stared straight ahead.

"No." She gave a rueful laugh. "Turns out, stakes can kill humans too."

Avila was silent for a moment. I could almost hear

the gears in her mind turning over. Her eyes never left Sun.

"What happened? Who'd ya kill?"

Sun shifted slightly before she faced Avila. She frantically rubbed the back of her neck.

"Avila," I started, shaking my head. "Leave it alone."

Avila didn't even look at me. Her eyes were like fire in water as she scrutinized our hitchhiker. It was Sun's brittle voice I heard next.

"Hawkers. There were three of them. They stumbled upon me in an old church I was squatting in. They'd been drinking rum ... and just as nasty as the devil's drink." She gave a half laugh and shook her head. "They'd been looking for some 'pink cookie', they said. For days, I couldn't stop them, couldn't leave, could barely breathe. On the fourth night, the ginger one got sloppy with his rope knot. I waited till the booze knocked them out cold and then I jimmied the rope from my wrists and drove this stake into each of their hearts."

Avila raised an eyebrow. She nodded briefly before turning her gaze toward the passenger window. Not much was said after that. We'd all been through our version of hell. Sun was right. Her story was no different to anyone else's.

The two women exchanged a few words every now then, but I tuned out for the most part. My thoughts were trained toward the rural landscape as it began to give way to desolate suburban streets that skirted the outer sections of the city. After hearing the disturbing scene Sun had just described at the hands of hawkers, I was having trouble pushing away visions of those barbarous humans pawing over my woman. Scarla must be beside herself with fear.

Swiney prickass lowlifes. If they so much as touched a hair of her head, I'll kill them all – one way or another.

I couldn't help but think of that last moment we shared on the beach together. The way the shade of her eyes deepened like copper inkwells when she looked at me. It haunted me. I'd failed her.

What if I couldn't get to her in time? What if it all went to shit?

I shuddered as feelings of helplessness and anger coursed through me. The hawkers had said they had a way of testing the blood type. If that were true, I couldn't produce anything other than the real thing. I had to keep my eye on the endgame. It was all I could do as I kept speeding through the streets, ignoring the stillness of the shopfronts, townhouses and buildings that only months before were part of a thriving city. Now, those dwellings were prey to vultures, crows and vermin that scavenged for human remains.

When the streets narrowed and the maze of

suburban districts began to merge with clusters of tall city buildings, I slowed the pickup in search for a discreet place to park. The hidden laboratory was in Norbury's southern precinct, about a mile and a half away. I didn't want to risk drawing unwanted attention by driving the truck through the inner-city streets. We would walk the rest of the way.

Scarla's favorite Italian restaurant caught my eye. We'd spent many an evening together drinking red wine and dining on boscaiola in that cozy joint. She loved it for its unexpected charm and authenticity. She loved it for its candlelit dining and checkered tablecloths. *Bella donna.* My gut knotted as peered closer at its gloomy facade.

Below the sloped faded green roof, the windows were covered in a slick of grime, the words "Bella E Buona" now barely visible. I recalled the off-street parking bay around the back of the small building. It was a perfect place to stow the pickup, and quite fitting given we were here for Scarla's sake.

I veered into the driveway and stopped the truck, the wrenching sound of the park brake shattering the silence in the cabin. I reached for my machete and the rucksack filled with rations and a water canister. I had also brought the hunting knives, a box of matches, a flashlight and a few candles. In the pickup tray, I stored a supply of fuel enough to get us back home. Avila and Sun gathered their belongings and climbed from cabin as I refueled the truck before setting off into the city.

Avila's boots scuffed the gravel parking bay as she crept around like a predator. She was clad from head to toe in black, her jeans appearing sprayed against her slim legs as she clutched the cleaver in one hand while carrying the swaddled stakes over a shoulder. She moved closer to me, gesturing toward Sun.

"What are we gonna do about her?"

I finished refilling the tank and twisted the cap into place before straightening to peer at Sun. She rummaged through her rucksack before producing a canister and taking a sip. As harsh as it sounded, she couldn't tag along with us. I could not risk jeopardizing the location of the laboratory.

"She will go her own way."

Avila gazed at Sun and nodded. I knew what she was thinking, but we had helped the woman reach her destination safely. There was nothing more we could do for her. We had our own problems and time wasn't on our side.

We parted ways with Sun and set off toward the lab. The hairs on my neck tingled as we hurried through the wasted city streets. It was as if time had frozen, leaving behind a collection of vacant buildings and harrowing steel in the wake of devastation. My breath shallowed as I thought about those who had died at the claws of the undead that hid in city basements and underground tunnels during the daylight hours.

A chill ran through me as we silently pushed forward, keeping our ears to the ground and our eyes trained on every street corner and abandoned car. You never knew what could be lurking in the shadows by day. Those brave enough to linger in the city with the bloodsuckers were just as dangerous as far as I was concerned. They were the ones who sought to strike a deal with the wicked. The ones who vowed to protect them while they slumbered. We called them the Shadow Guardians.

By the time we reached the building where the lab lay beneath ground level, the sun was swallowed behind the towering smoky glass and concrete buildings. The air cooled against the sweat on my brow and was tinged with the sickening stink of decomposing flesh. It wasn't long before my fingers ached from gripping the machete so hard.

I stalled at the entrance of the building as I cocked my head to gaze toward its mirrored veneer. It was a building I was familiar with, having visited its plush interior levels on many occasions in the course of my career. The laboratory had been created for covert government research purposes. And while I had never worked for the agency, I did periodically have dealings with their ongoing intensive research programs. I was initially led to believe their sole purpose was to find a cure for cancer and other blood diseases. However, it wasn't long before I became aware of the experiments with biological weapons that went on here. Particularly when presented with an in-depth confidentiality agreement.

I took a deep breath and turned to Avila. "Ready?"

Her eyes darted around the street before she looked at the huge glass doors leading into the lobby. She gulped.

"What if they're inside?" Her voice wavered as she turned back to me. "What if we wake them?"

I reached out to stroke away a strand of hair from her face. I forced a smile, but it evaporated as soon as it had emerged. It was possible we could be walking into a vampire lair and there was nothing I could say to comfort her.

I steeled myself and took another sharp breath.

"Get the stakes out and keep close to me."

5

DEAD AIR

The print of my palm smudged the slick of grime layering the heavy glass door as I eased it open. Dozens of contorted prints already smeared the surface. Avila's short breaths pricked the hairs on my neck as I peered into the lobby.

Dead air.

I scanned the dim spacious area. The foyer spread out in a flawless vision as my eyes darted, taking in the oversized couches and mahogany furniture among huge pots of faux greenery and sprawling rugs. On one side of the room, a vivid painting dominated the wall beyond a marbled countertop. On the other, rows of individual workstations lined the internal window-wall. My skin went cold as I spotted the solitary office chair lying overturned near the workstations.

My tongue suddenly felt like sandpaper as I inspected the black leather chair, which was the only evidence of the annihilated city beyond the heavy doors.

How had this building managed to escape the apocalypse?

It was an unsettling revelation. Other than that, I detected no movement in the lobby, but that didn't mean shit considering the vast space and dozens of upper floors I couldn't see from this viewpoint. My gaze trailed to the door leading to the building's stairwell which loomed unburnished and gray at the foot of the elevator corridor about fifteen meters away. I gripped the machete in one hand and a stake in the other, stealing myself to race to the door.

I glanced at Avila and gestured toward the stairwell. My voice was barely audible when I spoke. "Move fast and don't make a sound."

Her grim eyes nodded a reply. My heart lurched. I wanted to take her in my arms and hold her against my chest like I had when she was child. I wanted to make everything alright for her again. But it was a futile wish and wishes were yesterday's dreams. There were no words enough to take away the reality. She had become a child of devastation.

Our boots hardly touched the floor as we dashed through the lobby, keeping to the shadowed sections of the room before stopping short of the stairwell door. My chest constricted as I glanced down the darkened corridor where metal elevator doors glinted dully in the muted light offered by the grubby windows skirting the lobby. The unscathed appearance of the place heightened the mood of eeriness.

Something doesn't feel right.

I tried to suppress the thought and the accompanying shudder as I grabbed the door handle before slipping into the gloomy stairwell. The narrow shaft immediately seemed to close in all around me as an inkiness infected my bones. I paused to allow my eyes to adjust to the diminished light while Avila slinked in beside me.

She gagged. "Argh!" She clutched at my elbow. Her was voice low and shaky. "Death is here."

She was right. The stench was unmistakable. It was distinctive and sickly-sweet and as familiar as the rising sun. I reached for the flashlight stowed in the side pocket of my rucksack, flicking it on to illuminate an endless flight of concrete stairs broken by short landings as far as the light stretched. A frigid draft filled the stark shaft. There were four flights of stairs between us and the lab. *Four flights.* I prayed that death lingered in the opposite direction as I reached for Avila's trembling hand.

Her skin was cold against mine. She clutched the

stake in her other hand as if it were an extension of herself as she clung close to me through the dark. I gave her a squeeze.

"I'm okay, dad."

Her words tore into me as I wondered if bringing her along had been the right decision. *Was I leading her into a death trap? Would my choice forever change her destiny?*

There was no way for me to know and no time to second guess my decision. The alternative was to leave her alone at the cottage. Now that the hawkers knew where to find us, she would have been a sitting duck. I told myself that she was safer with me as I released her hand, ignoring the tension in every nerve of my body as I eased down the stairs toward the lab.

The building groaned and the shadows seemed to deepen with each step downwards. Like contorting, dark limbs, they writhed and expanded against the shaft of light from my flashlight before disappearing into the blackness we left behind. Avila's nails sunk into my waist as we crept along walls, her breath jagged in my ear while my senses went in overdrive. I pushed forward, progressing cautiously and with as much speed as I could, stopping when we reached the bottom of the stairwell to shine the light on the heavy metal door of the lab.

An odd sense of relief flashed through me as I skimmed the light around the bottom landing, seeing nothing but the gray slabs of concrete that enclosed the small area. The coast was clear but my fingers still tingled as they clutched the machete handle. I glanced at Avila and motioned toward the door.

"Come on."

I moved away from the wall as the sound of Avila's stake clanked against the floor as it slipped from her hand. My body froze as the sound reverberated along the steel balustrades, echoing up the lengthy shaft in a climatic staccato.

"Shit!" Avila cringed and scooped up the stake. She looked up.

I followed her gaze, catching sight of the balustrades glinting through the darkness as goosebumps covered my arms. My breath hitched at the faint sound of footsteps from above. Avila's gasp was followed by a sudden pinging noise at our feet. I looked down at a silver coin rattling against the concrete before coming to an abrupt stop.

Holy fuck.

Silence. I could barely breathe. Utter dread pulsed through me as I grabbed Avila's arm and dashed toward the door, gripping the handle at the same time that it opened an inch to reveal Michal's pasty face peering at me.

His dark eyes appeared spidery and wide beneath his glasses. His voice quivered.

"Jett?"

"Michal." I pushed on the door and ushered Avila into the lab, crossing the threshold as the cold draft carried the hideous sound of laughter. Two words clung in my mind.

Dead air.

6

RARE BLOOD

"Who or what the hell is out there?" Avila stalked between two long benchtops. She stopped to whirl around and glare at Michal. "You've set us up."

She had a point. It was clear we weren't alone.

Michal's bald skull gleamed dull beneath the emergency lights illuminating the laboratory. His finger's shook as he thumbed his glasses. "Wha – why would you suggest that, pigeon?"

Her eyes narrowed. "Don't you pigeon me, asshole." Her fingers tightened around the stake she waved with menace. She stepped closer to Michal who fidgeted beside me. "Who is up there, Michal? Have you become a Shadow Guardian? Are you their puppet now?"

He stiffened. His breath was hot and putrid as he slid closer to me, glancing between us. He began shaking his head and mumbling. I grimaced and stepped back.

My thoughts were erratic as I scanned the workstations, dormant machines and the dingy spaces cordoned off by glass panels. *Empty space.* My gut flipped. A faint whiff of human waste lingered in the stale air. I looked back at Michal.

"Where are the others?"

He shrieked and his arms flailed. His filthy white lab coat swung wildly as he paced the lab.

"Questions! Questions!" He stopped abruptly. Beady eyes dropped and followed the pattern his fingers sketched along a bench surface. When he looked back up, a layer of spit foamed his lips. "Did they send you here to interrogate me?"

Avila and I exchanged glances. Michal had always leaned on the eccentric side. It became obvious his mental health was strained. Horror. It teased out our weaknesses. My back ached. I didn't have time for this bullshit.

"Where is the rest of the team, Michal?"

There should have been six other scientists here. They were the group that had stayed behind to keep researching for a cure. I knew all of them. They were the brave souls that had lost their loved ones to the virus. That had vowed to never give up.

Michal's eyes darted around. His fingers tangled together as looked up at the ceiling. I followed his gaze. It was a stick-built grid system.

Some of the ceiling tiles were misplaced. I swallowed hard and increased my grip on the machete. He shivered visibly before he rushed toward me, his boots squeaking.

"They deserted me. All of them." His lips parted to reveal a set of stained teeth. He was about to say something else when was distracted by Avila who had begun stalking around the lab. She was headed toward the isolation spaces confined by glass panels. The experimental rooms were doused in darkness. Michal screeched as he set off after her.

"What are you doing?"

Avila ignored him. She stopped short of a glass wall to peer into one of the inky spaces. Her shoulders stiffened before she whirled around to catch my stare.

I noticed her expression pale over trembling lips. Michal halted somewhere between us, facing Avila as he began pulling at his ears.

Dead silence. My blood iced as Avila's gaze settled on Michal. Her boots dug into the floor as she planted them wide with her hand firmly holding the stake. She stared at him when she spoke.

"Dad, I think the team are still here."

Fuck.

My nostrils flared. I lurched forward as Michal began stumbling backward. He spun around. He blinked rapidly at me before he tried to escape. But he was already within arm's reach.

My blood ran hot as my finger's clamped into the back of his neck. He squealed as I yanked him toward me, and he struggled as I dragged him toward Avila.

She poised the stake at his chest. She looked at me and flicked her chin toward the glass panel. My knuckles tightened around Michal's neck as I leaned forward to peer past my transparent reflection into the glass.

Cold. It crept through me and jarred my senses. I shivered violently as I took in the grim scene confronting me. Blood was everywhere. It splattered across the floors and stuck to the chrome trolleys and benches.

Severed limbs and body parts splayed across a wheeled stretcher and appeared distorted through the darkness. My head throbbed. I tore my eyes from the dismembered bodies and clawed Michal's flesh. He yelped as I growled.

"What have you done?"

His skin felt damp. His stench was putrid. He

quivered and peered up at me, his words tripping over his tongue.

"Th – they were traitors." He shook his head, wincing as Avila pressed the stake into his chest. "The rare blood – I couldn't trust them – they all want it." He gestured toward the ceiling. His voice lowered. "What they say is true, Jett. The blood is power."

Avila twisted the stake into his coat. "Where is the damned blood, Michal? You told us it was here."

He became still then, his lips twisting into a grisly smile. "I hid it from them. I tricked the kindred." He laughed. "I had to kill them, Jett. If they had the blood and turned kindred, there would be no hope left to save what's left of humanity."

What the hell?

My thoughts reeled. I kept my grip firm. "The kindred are here?"

He nodded rapidly. "They've been here almost from the start. With some Guardians." He swallowed hard. "They call the overlord Marius. He let us live for the sake of our research. He's a cunning one ... smart. He has a vision to build a functioning society for the clans. Humans will be hunted down, seized and kept alive as prisoners to bleed at their own discretion."

"They need scientists ..."

"Yes! Specifically, hematologists."

Avila snorted. "That's why you're still breathing?" She dug the stake further into Michal's chest. Her eyes shadowed as he whimpered. "You've set us up. You've baited my dad here for them."

Michal shook his head furiously. "N – no, no. I might be many things, but I'm not a traitor!" He gave a rueful laugh. "I'm not suited for the world out there now." His gaze dropped to his arm as he slowly peeled back a grotty sleeve to reveal puncture marks trailing bruised skin.

Avila gasped. "It's already started."

Michal looked at me and reached into his coat pocket to produce a vial of blood. His fingers trembled. My stomach felt like metal as he spoke.

"You are the way to get the blood out of the city." He pushed the vial into my palm. "It's the gold our world knows now. It cannot fall into the wrongs hands, Jett."

I loosened my grip on him and took the vial. My head swirled and my body trembled as though with a fever. I glanced back at the dark room where the forsaken lay in torn pieces.

Michal was utterly insane. Yet, an exceptional mind still lingered beneath the madness long enough to keep the rare blood from the enemy.

Avila lowered the stake. The sound of light footsteps

drifted from the stairwell into the lab. Her eyes widened at me.

"They're coming."

Michal jerked. His eyes bulged as he gestured wildly toward the killing room. "Take the back-up stairs to the lobby. It's the door at the rear behind the benches and trolleys. Hurry!"

Back-up stairs? News to me.

There was no time to procrastinate. The sound of footsteps echoed down the stairwell shaft. I spun around with Avila as she flung open the heavy glass door and ran toward the back of the room where I spotted a discreet door beyond the stretcher and trolleys strewn with body parts.

I tried not to think about the blood or the blind eye sockets peering from mottled skin as I pushed Avila into the stairwell.

As I stepped into the dark, narrow space and began to ease the door closed, the sound of the laboratory door cracked as it flung open.

I paused to peer through the slit in the door now inches apart to see a figure shadowing the threshold. His hair was glossy and dark above a milky complexion and crystal-blue eyes. He wore black leather and chunky boots. A swathe of crimson hugged his torso.

My heart froze as he raised a jeweled hand to drum

talons against the door frame and flash his white fangs. But it was the sound of his silvery voice that sent my blood cold as I quietly closed the door.

"Michal, Michal. What are you cooking up down here, hmm?" He chuckled. "My daytime slumber has been disturbed with the news you have received some visitors. You know how protective I am of my sleep ..."

7

THE PROPOSITION

The vampire's image flashed through my mind. *Soulless eyes*. It wasn't even a thought. I was too pumped to think. My nerves felt stringy. My chest throbbed. I bounded up the stairs and every muscle strained. Sweat stung my eyes and almost blinded me as I shone the flashlight ahead. The stairwell was cramped, grotty and red. Dull scarlet lamps barely illuminated the landings. Human waste and stale iron snapped against my senses.

My breath was all I heard. *Or was it Avila's?* She took the stairs two at a time in front of me. My calves pounded. My ears buzzed. No time to think. Control was just beyond my grasp. We had to get out of here.

Three flights up, one to go. The door below creaked open, the faint sound grated into my heart. The jarred door blew in the sound of laughter. Lunacy. It was familiar. *Michal.* Avila stopped suddenly. She grasped the piped balustrade and swung around. Wide eyes peered at me through the dark as footsteps flew up the stairs behind us.

"Dad?"

I pushed a palm into her back. "Go!"

For Christ's sake – go!

The final landing loomed at the top of the stairs. Dark. Red. Hostile. My boots felt like a stampede. I pushed upwards. Avila was just about there. She yelped and tripped forward. I was so close behind her that she caught me in the offshoot. My chin slammed against her back and the machete slipped from my hand as I scrambled to get up.

I vaguely heard her behind me as she shifted to her feet and sprung onto the landing. The darkness was broken by a long hiss and golden eyes that glinted like firestones. Shallow breath. My fingers curled around the machete handle. I steadied my gaze to find him on the landing below me, golden hair like pink floss. Crimson lips appeared askew.

He leaned against the wall. His chin tilted and his lips twisted into a sinister grin. Shallow breath. My senses zoned in on him as I crouched on the stairs.

"Going somewhere without saying hello?" His voice

was a singsong. He tapped long talons together. "Tsk. Tsk. Would-be warrior humans, when will you ever learn?"

My eyes never left his. The clock was ticking.

His eyes narrowed to slits. His voice throaty.

"You cannot outsmart or outrun a vampire. Give me the vial."

Shit. They know we've got the blood.

I took a sharp breath and grabbed the machete as he lunged up the stairs. He moved like speed. The machete blade slashed at his chest as his talons caught me.

He slipped to his knees, grinning. Blood spilled over the blade as I stood and swung again. He leapt to feet, catching the thrust of the blade with his hand and tearing it from my grasp. The metal clanked on the stairs and a roar tore from his throat as he lunged at me.

Time stalled as I dodged his yellow fangs and talons. Avila's low shriek clung in my ear as she slipped from behind and jabbed her stake through his heart. His nails dug into my arm as he froze. His jaw dropped and his expression paled before he collapsed.

His body crumbled onto the stairs.

Holy fuck.

I spun around to see Avila panting. More footsteps came from below. No time to think. My arms burned. So did my lungs. I grabbed the machete. We bolted toward the lobby door, bursting across the threshold and sprinting through the vast dim space that separated us from the streets. There was sunlight in the street. Relative safety.

The distance appeared unfathomable. I kept my focus on the big lobby door. Avila ran silently beside me. Adrenaline burned through my system, dulling the pain. Fail and we were dead. Fail and the world would know even more evil.

My lungs silently screamed. Almost there. I reached for the chrome door handle and pulled. I heard a thump from behind. *What the hell?* Avila screamed beside me. My hand gripped the handle as I yanked on the door and turned to look for Avila. She was gone.

Sunlight flooded across the threshold and spilled into the lobby. I stood fast, jamming my boot against the heavy door as the warmth of the sun radiated over me. My chest heaved as my gaze darted around the lobby.

"Avila!"

"Dad!"

Her voice was followed by hideous laughter. That was when I saw her – trembling and ensnared between the claws of a vampire. My stomach dropped as I met her stare. They stood in the shadows along a wall painted gray that forked to give way to a series of long corridors. I hadn't seen him coming, and now, she was at his mercy.

The vampire's dark hair hung over his face and almost concealed eyes that glowed like neon lights as he held her firm. His fangs glistened only inches above her throat. She squirmed beneath his grasp and gritted her teeth.

"Let me go, asshole!"

He laughed, and his laughter was chorused by four other vampires as they emerged from the shadowy corridors to stand beside him. My heart felt like stone when I recognized Marius. It was defeat that gripped me.

I stood firm in the sunlight. I studied them as I struggled to gage the situation. The sun was neither friend nor foe in that moment. I wanted to burn to ashes as I beheld my daughter and took in her pallid expression and wild eyes. She swallowed visibly. Her eyes narrowed as she shook her head.

My little tough nugget.

I knew she meant for me not to yield to the bloodsuckers. Yet, I couldn't accept what that would mean for her. Hopelessness rimmed as Marius moved toward Avila. He clasped her hand and pulled her to him. His pale features were a striking contrast against his thick black hair as he regarded her before turning toward me, grinning.

"Jett, isn't it?" His brows raised as he looped an arm around Avila. He glanced down at her. "Such a beautiful daughter. Now, we both possess something that is precious to the other. What to do ..."

I stiffened and lifted my chin.

"Let her go, Marius. I have what you want."

"Step away from the sunlight and give it to me." He went to stroke a strand of hair from Avila's face but she turned her head away and looked at me.

"No, dad. Don't give it to them."

Marius laughed. His barnacle cronies joined in behind him. I wanted to kill them all.

"Hmm ... such fire!" Marius glanced at the others before giving Avila an approving nod. His gaze darkened when he looked back at me. "Quite an admirable trait, but one that will not keep her alive." He paused and took an exaggerated breath. "Tell you what; I have a proposition for you, Jett. I heard tell that you are an extraordinary hematologist – a skill I am in need of to help build the utopian world I have envisioned. Join us and no one needs to die today. In fact, no one need die ever. I'm offering you and your daughter the gift of eternal life. What do you say?"

I gaped at him as his words spiraled through my

mind. It was despair that found victory over my emotions as I looked at Avila. She stood defiant and brave in the face of evil. Her eyes focused on me and my heart shattered as the weight of the situation shadowed me. If I handed the blood over to Marius, he would possess the power to transcend into a vampire with extraordinary abilities. He and his clan would become all powerful; monstrous creatures of the night that would ravage the earth and take every living being with them.

I could feel my veins bulging beneath my skin as Avila's eyes dampened and she mouthed the word 'no'. My heart lurched. I shuddered as I strained to provide an answer to a choice I'd never dreamed possible.

Dreams were yesterday's wishes on charred wings. The survival of humanity now rested on my shoulders and my daughter's life.

My beautiful little nugget.

8

CRY TO ME

When your baby leaves you all alone and nobody calls you on the phone.

Silence is a noise. Ragged breaths and the soulful sounds of Solomon Burke's *Cry to Me* screamed through my mind as I stared at my daughter. It was her favorite. The moments stalled. *My child.* Images of her long dark hair bouncing over her shoulders as she danced clung in my mind's vision. Flouncing yellow dresses. Small ruby lips breaking into laughter. The sweet sound of her voice when she called to me.

My heart ached. Her dewy lashes glistened despite the nod she gave me. The world spiraled with nothing beneath my feet. The lobby door cramped against my boot. My toes were numb. The beat of the sun slammed against my back. I wanted to die right then and there.

Better that than to face the impossible choice confronting me.

Avila.

I was startled as Marius began humming the bluesy tune playing through my mind. My nerves spiked as I looked at him. His skin appeared luminous beneath the dull light as he spread his arms.

"Doncha feel like crying, Jett?" He looped his fingers beneath his chin, grinning. "Ah ... surprise, surprise! You weren't aware that some of us kindred have the ability to invade minds?" He laughed before snaring an arm around Avila. "It used to be my mother's favorite too. So, you see, we're going to be one big happy family!"

"Like hell we will!" Avila pushed against him, glaring. Her next words were delivered through gritted teeth. "You are a satanic brute."

She shrunk away as he hissed at her. Talons clawed at her hair. She didn't even whimper. Her jaw tightened as she glared at him. "Dick!"

He frowned at her with amusement before turning to me.

"I am growing very fond of your daughter. Her energy is ... intoxicating. Sometimes, we're not aware of what we're missing from our lives until we encounter it."

His grin dissolved as the noise of heavy footsteps came from the corridors behind him. "Play time is over.

Bring me the vial or I'll have the Guardians take it from you."

A group of people suddenly spilled from the shadows into the lobby. There were about eight of them; men and women clad in dirty denim and knee-high boots with whips slung at their waists. Black bandanas hugged their skulls and their expressions were cold.

I could barely breathe as I surveyed them.

"When you're all alone in your lonely room and there's nothing but the smell of her perfume."

Time stopped as my gaze rested again on Avila. She was motionless, her image already fading as I took a step back. She mouthed the words *"I love you"* and my heart splintered into a thousand pieces.

Marius shouted as the sound of thudding boots charged toward me. The Guardians were on the move. It was time. I tore my eyes from Avila and spun around, sprinting from the lobby threshold into the street.

The air was a hot enemy and pain already an unwelcome friend. I was suffocating. *Dying*. My boots were concrete as I pushed forward. *Get to the corner.* The Guardians yelled out behind me. Lurking shadows filling doorways, watching the scene unfold. Manic laughter flooded the street. The corner came closer. *Closer*. My legs felt like pudding.

In the blur of the moment came another sound. *A*

machine? An engine? My thoughts scattered. My tongue stuck to the roof of my mouth. *Breathe, Jett.* I fought for air. Go faster. My calves burned and I was blind. *Avila.* My ears pricked up through the deafening haze as a high-pitched screech crunched across the road.

Tires.

The muscles of my body tightened as I spotted the metallic blue Jeep come to a sudden halt at the corner. *What the fuck?* My pace instantly slowed. I could feel the tremors in my body as the window lowered and the Guardians shouted from behind.

"Get the bastard!"

"Hurry!"

I glanced over my shoulder as swollen faces closed in fast. My fingers grasped the machete. There was no time to think. I swung my eyes back to the Jeep and the face that was distorted beneath golden hair.

"Jett! Get in!"

Sun?

I squinted, hesitating before bolting for the Jeep and flinging open the door to the shouts of the Guardians skidding up behind me.

"The bastard's getting away!"

"Motherfucker!"

I was still about to shut the door when Sun slammed her foot on the accelerator and sped off down the street.

The Jeep engine roared and the hot wind gusted into my face as I yanked the door closed, my chest heaving as I stared back at her. Grimy slim fingers gripped the steering wheel. She chewed her bottom lip, glancing at me.

"Where's Avila?"

I squeezed my eyes shut as my body was racked with spasms. My throat hurt when I swallowed as I gazed ahead. All I could see was the image of Avila's bright lemon dress and her hair swinging as she danced.

I formed the words that tortured my soul. "She's gone."

Doncha feel like crying. Doncha feel like crying.

9

DEAD INSIDE

"Tea?" Sun's smile evaporated as fast as it had emerged. The dark circles beneath her eyes darkened. "You need to drink something ... eat something."

I looked at the steaming mug she shoved toward me. My fingers felt numb.

"My grandmother used to say that tea makes everything better." Sun gave a half laugh. When I stared back at her, she bit her bottom lip and looked away as she sat down on the sofa next to me. "Take it. You're going to need your strength."

I took the mug and pondered the hot milky broth. My grandmother used to say the same thing about tea. It was a lie. No amount of tea could ease the constant stabbing sensation crippling my stomach, nor could it erase the evil that took my lover and claimed my daughter. Tea wouldn't make everything alright.

I tentatively took a sip and forced the liquid down my throat, grimacing. It hurt to swallow. It hurt to breathe. My skin was chilled from the inside out and it was guilt that weighed heavy on my heart. I was alive. Avila was not. I had forsaken her for a future hung on false dreams and unfounded myths. I'd failed my daughter.

Dreams have no place in this new reality. Dreams are nothing but feeble whims on the devil's tongue. They mean nothing.

I set the mug down on the coffee table and stood up, running my fingers through my dark hair and sighing. *Dead.* Everything inside me felt bloodless. I barely glanced at Sun as I paced the cottage sitting room.

"You should go. The hawkers will be here before long."

"I already told you, I'm not going anywhere. There's nothing left for me."

There's nothing left for anyone.

I stopped at the window and peeled back the curtain, scanning the cottage porch and yard. My gaze settled on the dense twisted trunks bordering the gravel clearing as I contemplated her sudden appearance in my life. She had said she knew where to find me in the city the day before; that she'd followed us before discovering her daughter's remains perishing on the floor of her living room. She said she had guns.

I spun around to see her bottom lip trembling, but her azure eyes blazed. I sighed.

"Stay with me and you'll probably die before the end of this day."

She gave a rueful laugh and rubbed her palms over her jeans. Her eyes moistened.

"You are the kindest person left in this world. You helped me when nobody else would." She shook her head, her stringy golden hair clinging to her cheekbones. Her voice lowered. "I'll die with you today, Jett."

Her words were delivered with simplicity, yet they struck hard against my heart. I shook my head. I barely knew this woman and didn't understand her reasoning, but there was no need to. In a world overrun by vampires, swindlers and criminals, nothing made sense anymore. She was a ray of light in an eternal darkness. She *was* like the sun.

"Your parents named you well."

She smiled as our eyes briefly locked before I looked away and walked to where her guns lay on the floor. I picked up a long-barrelled firearm. My hands were clammy against the cold metal, but I felt a sense of comfort as I drew back the hammer and cocked the rifle before propping it by the cottage door. I'd never been overly fond of guns, nor had I owned one. Things were different now.

Sun stood and came up beside me. She selected a Glock 9mm handgun from the small stash of weapons and started inspecting the dull black short-barrelled pistol. Quick fingers ejected and reinserted the magazine before expertly gripping the handle and stuffing it in the pocket of her jeans. My curiosity was aroused but I said nothing.

"Where do you want me?" She flicked her chin toward the front door. "You want me to hide out in the trees?"

"No, they use the forest grounds as their cover. Stay by the window and keep out of sight. Train your gun on whoever has Scarla. If it goes to shit, kill as many of them as you can."

"With pleasure."

Scarla.

Just saying her name caused the shadow in my heart to deepen. I turned away and headed back to the window as my thoughts swirled with a thousand questions. *Had I done the right thing by leaving Avila at the mercy of vampires for the sake of preventing further mayhem and horror? Had I made the right decision? Was she dead already?*

Whether she was dead or not didn't matter in that moment – or even if I'd made the right decision. The choice had already killed me on the inside, and I knew I would never forgive myself whatever the outcome.

The only thing that mattered now was Scarla and her safety. Rare blood and super-powerful vampires be damned. One of my girls had to survive this ordeal. Whatever became of the blood would be out of my hands once I traded it to the hawkers for Scarla's return. I had to believe their hatred for the kindred would be enough to keep it from falling into their clawed hands. At least until I could realign and plan to retrieve it.

I was thinking all these things when a movement in the yard caught my eye. I instantly stiffened as a dozen hawkers slinked from the shadowy trees into the clearing. I motioned to Sun who nodded and dashed toward the other window facing the porch. She meshed her slim body against the wall and stole a glance through the curtains, gripping her gun close to her chest as the sound of boots thumped on the porch stairs.

My heart thundered. Sweat pooled across my brow as I scanned the group of hawkers and spotted the tall nasty looking one that had delivered their ransom conditions forty-eight hours ago. He was clad in the same get-up – faded leather and dirty boots. His teeth were like rust between ginger whiskers as he grinned, and he fingered his switchblade as he bounded up the stairs.

He banged on the flimsy door and at the same time, I saw Scarla. My eyes widened as she emerged from the trees with her feet dragging between two male hawkers who gripped her arms. Her pale hair hung over her face that was blotched with angry welts. Her swollen lips fell apart above a bruised jaw while her shredded clothes barely concealed her body.

What the fuck?

Rage took hold. Death was my friend. It was hot steel that claimed my blood and drowned out any coherent thoughts as I grabbed my machete before stomping toward the door and flinging it open to face my enemies. A sinister smile greeted me.

"Right on time." The gingered hawker gave a wry laugh. His weathered eyes dropped to the machete I gripped at my side. He twirled the switchblade. "What ya think you're gonna do with that, eh?"

Cut you all to pieces.

"Touch my woman again and you'll find out, asshole."

He growled and his eyes flashed at me before he glanced over his shoulder toward his mob. I braced myself and followed his gaze, taking in the leathered men carrying an array of weapons. Some carried swords in worn scabbards that swaddled their waists while others held blades and chains. Two hawkers stood at the foot of the forest doused in the shadows and pointing rifles at me. But it was the gangly looking man holding a hunting knife at Scarla's throat that really caught my attention.

Dizziness threatened to overtake me when she lifted her chin long enough to blink at me through bloated eyes. Her head lulled forward, the afternoon sun catching the blood staining her scalp.

"Scarla." Her name clung on my lips and panic seized me. I stepped across the threshold but ginger-beard sidestepped closer, blocking my way to the stairs.

A thick layer of grime crammed the wrinkles around his eyes as laughter erupted among the group. He cocked his head. His voice was gruff.

"Let's start over, shall we? If you'd like to avoid watching the tart bleed like a dirty pig today, I suggest you give me what I came here for."

My eyes stung as I glared at him and slowly reached into my pocket to retrieve the vial of blood that represented my daughter's death and Scarla's torture. The same drops of blood I knew would forever represent the death inside of me. Things were different now; everything felt bloodless.

"Marla!" Dark eyes flickered at me. Ginger-beard licked his lips as he clutched the vial of blood.

Void.

Some moments were barren of thought. His eyes bored into me. My mouth was a desert. A thin figure pushed through the hawkers crowding the stairs. A woman.

I glanced at her as she took the vial, pausing to look at me with a twisted grin. Her skin appeared cracked and discolored beneath the dull shine of the studs and hoops adorning her face. Her gray eyes were cold.

"How long?" Ginger-beard said.

"Six minutes." Marla pulled a small box from her

jacket pocket – a blood test kit. She dropped to her knees and began fidgeting with it with tremulous fingers.

Ginger-beard scraped the end of his switchblade across calloused knuckles and grunted a reply. Scarla sobbed as hawker fingers knotted in the hair at her nape. A rusty blade balanced at her throat. She trembled as she looked back at me. *Torment*. It killed. I could barely control the pain. The sound of his voice was like salt on a wound.

"People like you always thought you were superior to everyone else. White collar bullshit blinders. Used to get around like your shit didn't stink in your cars and shiny suits." He gave a half laugh. His breath was a stench. "I'm not a bloodsucker lover, but I can't help but take satisfaction in how things have turned out ... I always believed that one day people like you would get what's coming to ya; white collar crimes finally caught up when your biological poison went wrong."

He leaned closer. "Justice. That's what that is. You people were so caught up in your own asses that you never saw it coming, did ya? Where did all that education and privilege get ya at the end of the world, eh?"

I tightened my grip on the machete.

"I'm still here, fucktard."

He laughed. "I'm looking at a dead man walking.

You don't have what it takes to see this out. This world isn't made for your kind anymore."

The hawkers lingering on the stairs chuckled but I ignored them as Marla stood up suddenly. She waved a piece of cardboard between filthy fingers. The silver rings on her brows lifted.

"Score!"

My breath quickened.

Void.

Some moments seemed endless. I swung my eyes back to ginger-beard. A pasty yellow tongue stuck out as he grinned.

"Well, well, the blue-eyed white neck delivered after all."

My throat felt like sharp glass.

"That's right. You've got your ransom." I flicked my chin. "Leave the woman and get the hell off my property."

His eyes pierced into me. "You might just have a half decent set for a club-fed." He gave a snigger and my blood ran cold. Marla laughed.

His voice filled my head. "Bleed the pig!"

Void.

Some moments swallowed you whole. My brain felt like an acute explosion as the hawker yanked Scarla's head back. The sound of her cry blasted in my ears as the rusty blade sunk into her throat and slid across her skin, releasing a flood of blood from the jagged wound.

"Scarla!"

I roared and swung the machete as I charged forward, collecting Marla in the back of her skull just as she spun around to move away. The blade cracked against bone. Manic gripped me. I drove the shank forward with the thrust of the motion as loud cracks rang out across the yard. The sound of the gunfire instantly purified my mind.

Clarity.

Some moments feel as if you see the following scene unfold before it happens. Time slowed. Marla dropped to the floor as the hawkers on the stairs lunged forward, propelling blades and swinging chains ahead of them.

Fuck.

More shots fired. My ears buzzed. I jabbed the machete in front of me, piercing leather as a stabbing pain detonated in the side of my gut. My flesh felt like sponge. The odor of blood mingled in the air along with the shouting hawkers. Pain was a welcome friend beneath the repeated strikes of ginger-beard's switchblade. I stumbled back, instinctively reaching to quell the wound as I managed to stabilize my footing.

My fingers were warm, sticky. My head began to spin. Ginger-beard cackled like an old hag. Sinister.

Wicked. His ugly face contorted before me as I swung the machete. The effort was lost as the end of a chain caught around my wrist. Metal stung my flesh as the machete clanked to the timber floor and gunfire reverberated over the cottage. The sound of squawking birds mixed with laughter. I balled my fists and launched a right hook at a converging hawker. A blade plunged into my gut. Images distorted.

Scarla.

My heart felt like a blackened husk as I doubled over. My boots were awkward. I stumbled again. Sweat dripped into my eyes. Or was it blood? I couldn't breathe. My hands clenched my stomach as my head filled with pain.

Thwack! A white flash zapped behind my eyes. Then I was spiraling. My legs gave way and I fell hard to the brutal blows of dirty boots and blunt chains.

Void.

Some moments are not spent within our fleshy exteriors. I drifted away. Darkness beckoned as gingerbeard bent over me to trace the switchblade across my cheek.

"I was wrong about you, white neck." He paused the blade, digging the pointy end into the flesh just below my eye. "You ain't got nothing between your legs that your high-end pussy didn't have. We did her real good.

She was a running train and screamed just as loud as one." He gave a throaty chuckle and stretched to his feet. "I'll let you think about that while you bleed. We did ya solid."

The image of receding boots doubled as numbness took hold. A chill ran across the back of my neck and radiated through my body. My eyes felt heavy. *Heavy.* A whirling sensation overtook and then there was nothing.

Void.

11

SCORE

"*D*ance with me."

"*I'm an awful dancer.*"

"*You're wrong. Your soul dances with mine every day.*"

There are some places you can't remember but can't forget. She had a secret; a garden filled with precious blooms and wild roses. *Eden.* I had never known a love so deep; so pure. *She was a gift on earth.* Now, she was nothing. Her dreams were invisible dust on lost memories. Scarla was gone.

"Bella donna." I didn't recognize my voice as I hunched over the steering wheel of the pickup and struggled to focus on the road. Sun groaned. The sound of her voice startled me as her head lulled on my lap.

I glanced down at her, flinching as the moonlight

struck golden hair stained crimson. Our blood mingled. My hands were tacky as I reached to stroke her forehead. Her skin was ice. "Almost there. Stay with me."

Her body lay curled up on the pickup bench seat. She was limp and pitted from the bullets that had hit her. Her lips were tinged blue as her jaw slackened beneath fluttering eyelids.

"Wha – where are we going?"

I barely heard her above the rumbling engine as we careened through city streets. The broken white lines on the road flashed against the headlights like apparitions. *Death is unforgiving.* I was clawing at its door. *Stay or go?* Nothing left to breathe for; nothing except the score. It's strange how we find our greatest strength when looking down the barrel of oblivion.

"We're going to level the score."

My body felt raw. I was butchered and bleeding. It hurt to breathe and my mind was a hazy impression of honey-amber eyes and sensuous plump lips. *The place I can never remember; the place I'll never forget.* Grief lingered somewhere above me. Or perhaps it was grief that froze my heart and overrode my senses as the pickup skidded around the final corner, but it was hatred that motivated me when I slammed my foot on the brake outside the building.

An eerie quietness shrouded the cabin when I killed

the engine. The moments stilled as I peered ahead at nothing. *Nothing.* I didn't see the darkness flooding the street nor the towering shadows cast by the buildings. All I saw were fading memories of a life I would never know again.

Sometimes, the choices we make aren't ours to decide. Sometimes, the path forces us to unfathomable places. My choice to come here felt as if it was out of my hands. I'd come here for retribution. I'd come to do the unthinkable; to pledge the remainder of my days to darkness, violence and yield to the thirst of blood. I'd come here to be undead. But I couldn't make that choice for Sun. She had to choose for herself.

I gazed at her as she drifted in and out consciousness. She was pasty. Her breath was shallow and erratic. Like me, she wouldn't survive her wounds for much longer. My tongue felt thick as I swallowed and tried to rouse her, stroking back a lock of her hair and speaking her name. She groaned softly.

"You're a survivor, Sun. A ray of light in a world of fear and shadows." I paused as she opened her eyes to gaze up at me. I forced a smile. "You have to choose now – death or eternal life in death."

Her lashes clung together as she blinked and stiffened. Her bottom lip slackened before she lifted a hand and reached for my chin, wincing.

"J -Jett?"

I cupped my hand over hers and leaned my chin against her palm, squeezing my eyes shut as my heart shredded along with the blood oozing from my gut. Her skin was clammy and cold. Yet, the gesture was profoundly comforting and among the last I would ever know in my humanity. When I looked back at her, she merged with the tears blinding my eyes.

Her lips quivered as she inhaled sharply.

"I'll die with you tonight, Jett." She flinched and coughed. Her eyes dimmed as she looked at me again. "I'll go where you go."

I pressed my lips to her forehead. "Whatever happens, don't let them take your soul."

The sounds of unearthly screams caught in the still of the night and echoed along the street. My ears pricked and I felt my pulse quicken. I felt a sense of detachment as I climbed from the pickup and scooped Sun in my arms.

Cold.

I felt like a ghost despite the warm air that blew as I carried Sun toward the lobby doors of the building where I'd left my daughter the day before.

Weight. My knees almost buckled beneath the strain. I welcomed the pain. My veins throbbed but I relished the last of the fading warmth beneath my skin. I barely heard the distorted cries and harrowing shrieks carried on the slight breeze as they became closer. *Closer.*

The shadows came alive as dark figures emerged from the darkness. I balked as I clung to Sun and looked at them. Neon eyes glinted back at me from pallid expressions and milky skin. Scarlet lips curled up to reveal the dull gleam of fangs; hair glossed over shoulders clad in satiny attire as they regarded me. One of them started to move closer.

She regarded me from under a veil of vibrant red hair that cascaded to her waist. She reached out to stroke a talon across Sun's cheek before flicking her cat-like eyes at me. Full lips broke into a grin.

"Welcome to the Mysticus clan, your daughter awaits you."

12

BLACK HEART

Black hole. Black heart. Black everything.

I looked up at the night sky. Silvery clouds stretched across the half moon and the stars shone like cryptic messages. Bats soared on silent wings while the sounds of night creatures echoed in my ears. Nothing had changed. Yet, everything had changed. No single element appeared the same to my vampire senses. Everything was accentuated. Everything was striking.

"Are you ready, dad?" Avila's eyes flashed electric blue through the dark. Her skin appeared luminous and as pale as the clouds overhead as we stood at the foot of the forest assessing the cabin in the clearing.

The torment swirled in my gut and almost quelled the thirst biting at my veins when I looked at her. *My girl*. Ribbon laced braids and days at the fair. Lipstick on prom night. The way her eyes turned green before she was about to tell me a lie. Warm blood and a human heart. My girl had died and I wasn't there for her. She had been reborn into the cold-blooded beings now dominating our world. She was now a vampire. It was time to level the score.

I gave a slight nod and glanced at Sun who stood next to Avila. Her golden hair tumbled over shoulders clad in black leather. It was just as lustrous as the eyes gleaming back at me. Her long talons clung at her hips as her gaze deepened.

"Are you sure you want to do this?"

My jaw tightened.

"Yes."

Boisterous laughter erupted from behind the weathered timber walls of the cabin as the door flung open. A hawker male swayed as he gripped the balustrade to steady himself before making his way down the stairs. His voice slurred when he mumbled. Whiskey and tobacco mingled with the sickly odor of week-old sweat and carried on the breeze. His boots dragged across the clearing toward a tree. He belched repeatedly as he fiddled with his fly. The sound of his beating heart was intoxicating. I groaned inwardly and stepped forward, stopping when Sun grabbed my arm. Her fangs glinted with her hiss.

"Marius will kill you."

My veins bulged with the venom coursing through me. It took everything I had to tame the rage. I reached for her hand. Cold on cold. Darkness accompanied apathy. It was consuming. I held her gaze. My lips barely moved when I replied.

"He already has."

I released her hand and spun around before sprinting toward the hawker. The shadows were a part of me; the breeze was my ride. Blood was my lover. I stopped behind him and tilted my head to the side, watching as he stiffened before slowly cranking his neck around to look at me. Spidery eyes widened as I grinned.

"Hello, friend."

He gasped. The tips of his filthy beard fell as he stumbled back.

"Wha – what the hell?"

"Suitable word."

Black hole.

I could feel the pressure splintering in the pit of my stomach. My pulse throbbed desperately. I ensnared a hand around his throat. My talons cut into his skin as I rolled back my lips, hissing. My movements were effortless. The sound of his wail distorted in my ears when I flung my jaw forward to sink my fangs into his flesh, instantly relishing the taste of the blood he offered. His pulse was ecstasy.

Sweet. Salty. Warm.

In the cold-blooded creature I'd become, it was the warmth I craved above all else. But there was not enough blood to bring back my humanity. There was not enough vengeance to bring back Scarla nor return Avila to her mortality. But there was the blood of dreams and dreams were yesterday's wishes – and those wishes were my retribution.

I'd come here for more than just the blood of the hawkers that had killed Scarla. I had come with the promise of returning to Marius the rare blood he so desperately sought to possess. Promises made by the undead remained undead.

A growl tore through my throat as I released the hawker. He slumped at my feet. His blood coursed into my being. Elation gripped me. I felt my eyes blaze as Avila and Sun watched silently, the hunger in their stare unmistakable. I nodded and licked my lips.

"The ginger-beard is mine. No survivors."

Demons. That was the word circling in my mind as we took the steps onto the cabin porch before crossing the threshold into the sitting room. Demons for the merciless creatures we had become and for the treacherous acts we now bestowed upon surviving humans. We had become what I had despised the most – slaves to the darkness and forever damned.

Avila and Sun stood either side of me as we paused to take in the scene. About a dozen hawkers sprawled on the lounges and lingered around the edges of the room, cackling. One of them sat on the floor and strummed an old guitar. Smoke curled from makeshift ashtrays and glowing pipes. Through the haze a withered coffee table crammed with bottles of whiskey and dirty glasses was the center of their world.

Black heart.

Silence fell as they became aware of us. Promises of death foreshadowed. It had never sounded so pleasing. My nostrils flared as I inhaled fragrant gifts. Sour pickings. Riffraff lineage flowing in sanguine fluid beckoned as I curled my upper lip and my eyes settled on ginger-beard.

His dark eyes flashed as he stood up. The machete he fingered was familiar. Sweat formed across his brow and clung to the tips of his beard as he squared his shoulders, facing me. The machete balanced ahead of him.

Some of the hawkers gathered beside him; others cried out and made for the doors leading to other parts of the cabin. There was no place they could hide.

My gaze rested on the machete.

"What do you think you're gonna do with that, hmm?"

Ginger-beard swallowed. His heart thumped in my ear.

"I shoulda known you was a traitor to your kind." He shook his head. "Club-fed pussy. Taking deals with the devil and feeding on the blood of the innocent. This was the only the way you could make it in the new world."

"Perhaps you're right." I stepped forward. "But sometimes the people claiming to be our kind force us to make choices we never dreamed possible."

He took a sharp breath. His fingers tightened around the machete handle. Avila and Sun began to advance. The hawkers standing next to him started to back away. Ginger-beard's lips trembled.

"You came here for the blood – you can have it!" His fingers shook as he reached into his jacket pocket to produce the vial. "Take it – but hear this, blood-sucker – the time will come when the earth will know reckoning; an era when the Blood Legend will appear to right the wrongs of your kind and claim vengeance on all kindred. You will fall and you will fail." He tossed the vial at me. "And I'll be laughing from my grave."

I gave a half laugh. Failure already blackened my heart. I slipped the vial in my pocket before lifting my arms in a sweeping gesture. When I spoke, my voice was hollow.

"Bleed the pigs."

Black everything.

I lunged for ginger-beard as he swung the machete. The blade pierced my stomach but I felt nothing. His hair was like matted straw as I gripped his forehead. Bloodshot eyes swelled and brimmed from sunken sockets. Screams and wails reverberated across the room. Avila and Sun screeched as talons tore through flesh and fangs sunk into skin. I dug my fingers into his face. He didn't even struggle as I looked into his eyes and gave him a black smile.

"You stole a part of my soul and now I'll take yours with me to hell."

I roared before abruptly twisting his head between my hands. The sound of bone crunched beneath the impact, but I didn't stop. I couldn't stop. A red haze filled my vision as I tore his head from his neck in one fluid action. Blood sprayed over me. My eyes closed and I saw Scarla.

Warm honeyed eyes. Long dark lashes. Soft skin, platinum locks and sensual hips. Lips and love; my love. *Bella donna.* She smiled and reached for me as my heart cracked and my soul yearned for one last touch – one final kiss. And then she was gone, and everything was black and bloody, and curdling cries filled the air as I looked at the unfolding massacre.

Black everything.

I turned away and left the cottage. I bolted through the forest. My feet were like wings. My heart pumped darkness. I stopped at the edge of the sea to gaze down at the footprints that spread like golden illusions beneath the pale moonlight.

My fingers felt like steel as I reached for the vial of rare blood; blood that had the power to transform me into something more powerful than any other vampire on earth. The same blood that took my girls.

I removed the lid from the vial, dropped to my knees and gazed at the dark sea. The cold water rushed all around me with the incoming tide. I felt nothing. *Nothing.*

"Did you ever want to step into someone else's feet?"

Scarla's voice taunted the edge of my soul as I recalled the last of our conversations.

"Don't you mean shoes?"

"No."

I threw the vial into the receding waves and called her name. My voice was instantly stolen in the wind.

"Thousands of footprints have marked this beach over just as many years; I'd give anything to step in any one of them."

I stretched to my feet. Her name was a whisper on my lips as I began following the prints back up the beach toward the road.

"*But then you wouldn't be here with me in this moment.*"

Prints that would haunt me forever.

Jett's story is set to continue in *Blood Legends: Rebirth* and will be available to grab right now! Meanwhile, see below for an EXCLUSIVE preview – the first chapter of the original *Blood Legends* Series!

Blood Legends: Undead is a part of Kim Petersen's *Blood Legends* series. If you loved this story and want to be alerted when the next *Blood Legends* book is released, follow the link to subscribe to get exclusive *Blood Legends* email-alerts straight to you: Email-alerts

ABOUT THE AUTHOR

Kim Petersen is a USA Today Bestselling Author, author of *The Ascended Angels Chronicles*, and co-author of the *Stone the Crows* series. Her debut novel, Millie's Angel received a gold award in the 2017 Dan Poynter's Global eBook Awards.

Join Kim's Reader Tribe and Grab a Free Read:

https://forms.aweber.com/form/72/1801730872.htm

Find Kim at:

Whispering Ink: https://whisperinginkpress.com/

facebook.com/kimpetersen11

twitter.com/kimpetersen_

2070 - THREE STREAMS VILLAGE

Ten miles west of the Norbury City Ruins

Blood is treated like wine, or so I had heard from those fortunate enough to have lived to tell of cadaverous creatures. I lived in a hidden village nestled within the walls of an intricate web of caves miles from the ruined city. The elders called the village Three Streams because it intersected with three flowing, fresh rivers. They call us the Leavings. We are among the last surviving humans on earth, the ones the Vampiric Virus had left behind decades ago. About fifty Leavings called Three Streams home, needless to say it wasn't a shortage of water that threatened our existence. It was the kindred clans stalking us for the blood pushing through our veins that jeopardized the survival of humanity. We had become pawns between two vampire clans plaguing the land with a bloody war fought beneath the cloak of a night sky.

The vitality of the velvety, plasma-rich liquid that pumps through vessels, and fuels the hearts in all living creatures cannot be disputed. Without blood, humans could not exist. Now, blood has turned into a deadly, fast-moving commodity, during days when pale faces, cyclopean eyes, and sharp fangs reign supreme over the earth. Vampires now dominated the earth; humans had become the minority.

Some called me a Blood Legend. Those words weighed heavy on me. I resented every syllable. My parents had even named me Eva because of the rare blood flowing through my veins. Eva means 'life'. My parents were convinced that my blood, and the blood of my younger sister Kaia offered the life-force, the solution, perhaps, the legacy for the resurrection of humanity.

The birth of every Leaving child is followed with a simple blood test our predecessors had salvaged from the ruined city, that's how we come to know our blood types. It's how they'd discovered that Kaia and I happened to possess the world's most sought-after blood. The AB-positive blood type was rare even before the Vampiric era. Now, it had become priceless. The two clans that governed the ruined city lived their every moment in pursuit of our blood. Above all else, the Mysticus Clan and the Cruentus Clan scoured the desolate ruins for those with our blood type. It was their nucleus, the lore of their kind. The prize that would provide its host the power to defeat the other clan forever.

I guess you could say we were special.

Special was the last thing I felt right now, though. Beads of sweat stung my dark eyes and clung to my lashes as I wiped my brow with the back of my hand and clasped my wooden Samurai training sword with my other. Then I feigned a sigh, dropping my chin while gazing up at my sensei as if in defeat.

Astrid circled me warily. Her tightly bound ponytail hung glossy like liquorice under the morning sun as her supple feet glided along, her sword poised in slender hands. Her lips stretched briefly. I knew she thought she had me worn down for the session, but that's what I wanted her to think.

"Had enough, sunshine?"

She swivelled her sword between her fingers. The smooth timber saber followed her fluid movements gracefully.

I shrugged and grinned back, mirroring her motion with my own sword.

"Is that sweat glistening in your hair?" I asked. "Have *you* had enough, *sunshine?*"

Astrid was the type of person who made everything seem effortless. I had barely seen her break out in a smile, much less a sweat.

"I've had enough of your mouth," she said, scowling.

Her lips tightened as she moved like a firebolt and swung her sword toward my head.

I ducked and spun my boots in the earth while bringing my own sword around fast to connect with the back of her knees. I just caught the fleeting grimace on her face as her legs went slightly concave and she stumbled back.

I flashed her a wide grin and squinted at her brow line.

"It's sweat," I said, nodding before glancing around the training yard and spotting my best friend, Thayer.

He was sitting on a sandstone boulder at the side of the training range, sharpening a stake and watching the session. His thick eyebrows lifted with his grin as he paused to smile at me.

My small, sweet victory didn't last. I should've known; I had just broken the cardinal rule of combat. I had taken my eyes off my opponent, and this one had a nature like a Pit Bull Terrier out for blood. Astrid didn't take well to any kind of defeat.

In a matter of seconds, she was on her feet, her sword thrown aside in the dirt while her black almond eyes bore holes into the back of my head. I could've sworn I felt the heat of her stare at the same time as Thayer's face darkened in warning. But I was too late. She had already caught me in a headlock and I was crashing to the ground beneath her suffocating grip.

As much as I hated to admit it, Astrid was an excellent fighter, and highly disciplined in the principles of an array of Japanese martial arts. That's why Hendric, our village leader, had assigned Kaia and me under her care following our parents' disappearance. It was imperative that every village member learned to defend themselves to the best of their abilities, but considering our rare blood, Kaia and I had the most gruelling training regimen of all.

As I squirmed under Astrid's unrelenting, vice-like brace, I was certain the word 'care' might have been a little misleading in describing Hendric's selection of her as our guardian. The woman was nervy and as fearless as a summer storm. Seldom had I experienced her softer side, but I knew it was there somewhere – hidden beneath her hard-ass, Japanese exterior. Well, I thought it had to be.

"Enough now?" Her voice whisked into my ears like

a warm gush of wind while her bony elbow pressed under my chin. It didn't feel so good.

I stamped my fists into the dirt before I choked to death, and glared at her as she released me and offered her hand.

"You looked away."

"Yeah," I muttered, taking her hand and rising to my feet next to her.

She shook her head, the ends of her long raven hair sweeping across her shoulders.

"Why?"

My eyes darted to Thayer and then back to her. I shrugged as I tried to push away the beginnings of a blush. I failed.

Her brows lifted, but she didn't say a word. Instead, she took her stance before me and we bowed to one another, formally signalling the end of our session. I was grateful to graze my eyes over my feet for a few seconds.

By the time I'd straightened up, she was walking away from me.

"Now you can go to the fields and collect the supply of cabbages for the village before they turn," she called over her shoulder.

"What? Why?"

It wasn't my job to tend to the fields. When I wasn't on scouting expeditions, I took care of collecting fresh water and making sure our village barrels were always topped up.

Astrid whirled around and gave me a stern look. "Because collecting cabbages might remind you that distractions are a weakness in combat."

I rolled my eyes and loosened the elastic holding back my hair. I could feel a headache coming on.

"Seriously? I'm twenty years old. I think I know how not to be distracted in combat."

"Go tell that to the cabbage," she quipped before striding away.

My face screwed up with my scowl. Then I spotted Beck emerging from the clearing with his buddies, a smirk firmly impressed across his sharp features. My face began to ache at the sight of him.

"Got secrets for the cabbage, Eva?" he asked, picking up a training sword for his session. "I'll bet I know what your secrets are all about."

I was definitely feeling a headache coming on now. My fingers dug into my hips as I faced him, my jaw clenched. "I'll bet I know how to beat the living shit out of *your* secrets," I snarled, tossing my long, dark-amber braid.

He dropped the sword lower, holding it loosely by his side as he stalked closer to me. The ends of his short-cropped, sallow hair caught the sun and glowed over his scalp. His thick lips twisted.

"You wanna go there with me, cabbage-patch?"

I inflated my chest and squared my shoulders. No way was I going to back down from this dick.

"Anytime."

His brown eyes narrowed on me as he contemplated his options. We both knew I was the better trained fighter, yet he was a good foot taller than me and possessed a male's strength – which I obviously did not. Still, would he risk losing face in front of his friends?

We didn't have to find out because, suddenly, Thayer was practically stepping on my toes and pressing his nose against Beck's as he pushed himself between us.

"Alright, alright. Save your beef for our real enemies, you two!" he said, gesturing to the beyond with a nod. "You know those bloodsuckers are out there. Let's not lose sight of that fact."

His dark hair fell to the side while his inky eyes focused on me. I guess he did have a point, even if the three of us had never actually seen a vampire.

Beck shook his head as he began to wander away with a shrug. "Maybe she needs to talk to the cabbage about them vampires before she ends up their main blood-cow. I hear cabbage helps with *distractions*," he added.

I scrunched up my face and gave him my filthiest look as his friends gawked and laughed behind him. *Asshole.*

"C'mon, I'll help you in the field, *cabbage-patch.*' Thayer said, tugging on my arm.

I yanked my arm free.

"Eat shit, I'll do it myself!" I scowled, before storming away.

His laughter echoed behind me, his footsteps thudding in the earth as he gripped my wrist and pulled me to a stop. I whirled around with a belly full of anger and a whole lot of words ready to fling at him, but all of it melted somewhere at my feet when I caught sight of the smile in his eyes. I tried to ignore my flipping stomach as he squeezed my hand with his next words.

"I don't want to eat shit."

"You're an idiot."

He shrugged.

"Takes one to know one."

I laughed, shaking my head as I allowed him to lead me from the training grounds with his words still circling through my head. Vampires *were* the real enemies. Gone were the days of a world brimming with vibrant city lights and fast cars, when movies graced the screens of every household and fresh food was available at every street corner. That was a time when people could walk the city in safety, day and night. A time that preoccupied my daydreams and stirred an indescribable longing within me. But those days would forever elude me – they were stolen away long ago when the Vampiric Virus violated the world.

Nobody knows the real origins of the Vampiric Virus. Some say it was an experiment gone wrong. Others are convinced it began with a conspiracy. I think the real truth died along with the source. Either way, the rancid virus leached into the bloodstreams of millions like a merciless curse, leaving most of the population either infected or killed by the thirst of newborn vampires.

I had been trained to kill vampires from the moment I could walk, and I knew it was only a matter of time before they'd spill this far west. With that thought, I stifled the sudden giddiness in my belly.

Would I be ready to face the undead when the time came?

I wasn't so sure.

The air hung like a heavy blanket as we snaked deeper into the woods and trekked silently through a shroud of trees until the damp forest canopy gave way to a stretch of fields edging along a cliff-face.

I tramped through rows of cabbages and cauliflower until I reached the edge of the escarpment, where I dropped to my knees and squinted against the sun, breathing in the thin, warmer air blowing up from below. The ruined city of Norbury spanned out like a haze in the far distance. From here, the crumbling city appeared lazy and peaceful, much like a painting on a canvas. But I knew that was a farce. It was death and evil that lurked beneath those desolate buildings during the daylight hours.

As my eyes rested on the massive dome structure looming over one half of the city, I shuddered. The chrome sphere glistened bright under the reflection of the sun. My stomach began to churn. Thayer was right; it would be foolish to lose sight of our real adversaries. And I didn't know which clan was worse – the Cruentus Clan living and hunting in the ruins or the meticulously organized Mysticus Clan that farmed humans for blood under the protective UV dome structure beneath which they lived.

Blood Legends: Undead is a part of **Kim Petersen's Blood Legends** series. If you loved this story and want to be alerted when the next *Blood Legends* book is released, follow the link to subscribe to

get exclusive *Blood Legends* email-alerts straight to you:
Email-alerts

~

Join Kim's Reader Tribe and Grab a Free Read:

https://forms.aweber.com/form/72/1801730872.htm

Find Kim at:

Whispering Ink: https://whisperinginkpress.com/